The Big Race

Written by Jon Hinton

Illustrated by TADO

SCHOLASTIC

Bolt was very, very, **very excited.**
He had been training for weeks to be the fastest, speediest,
most zippiest monster in the whole of Trucksville.
And today was the big day. Today was the Trucksville Race!

Bolt joined the other Monster Trucks at the starting line.

Racing against Bolt were...

Fizz

Chunk

Roxy

Newton

and Masher.

"5... 4... 3... 2... 1...

...Go!"

RoA**RRRRR!** The six monsters zoomed along the
rainbow-coloured track. Masher was in the lead,
but Bolt was gaining fast...

PARP! A cloud of smoke shot out of Masher's exhaust pipe. **SCREEETCH!** Bolt slammed on his brakes.

"Yuck! Masher has been eating baked beans again!" coughed Bolt as he rejoined the race, now in last place.

Bolt was soon gaining on the other monsters.

Oh no! There was something in the road blocking his way...

SCREETCH!

Bolt slammed on his brakes... again.

It was Chunk!
"Hey buddy," cried Chunk. "There's something wrong with my wheel – can you help me?"
Bolt wanted to get on with the race but he couldn't leave his friend stuck here like this.

Bolt found a spike sticking out of Chunk's wheel.
He clenched the spike in his teeth, reversed and out it came.

POP!

"Thanks!" smiled Chunk.
"You're a great friend —
now let's race!"

Bolt zoomed past Newton and Masher...

...then past Roxy and Fizz. And yes – Bolt was in the lead! Bolt was about as happy as a Monster Truck could be.

He loved nothing better than racing.

"weeeeeeeeeeEEE!"

Bolt yelled as he whizzed along the track.

Then Bolt spotted another monster in trouble...
SCREEEEEETCH!
Bolt slammed on his brakes...
Yes —that's right—again!

Roxy was hanging off a cliff.

"Hold on Roxy, I'll save you!" shouted Bolt as he searched for something to tie around her. But there was nothing.

What could he do? The ground was giving way fast. If he didn't find something soon, Roxy would fall.

"Need any help, buddy?" came a booming voice behind Bolt.
Chunk turned around and showed Bolt his gigantic bottom.
Bolt was confused, but then he saw it — Chunk's tail!

Bolt clipped Chunk's tail to Roxy and they heaved her to safety.

"Phew —
thanks guys!"
laughed Roxy.

The three Monster Trucks zoomed along the
zig-zagging mountain road.
"We'll never catch the others now," said Bolt sadly.
"I really thought I had a good chance of winning."

"I wanted to win too," sighed Roxy. "But we've had an amazing day... and let's not give up quite yet!"

Bolt soon cheered up. After all, it was difficult to feel sad while racing through the Fountain Mountains. "Not long to go now," cried Roxy. "Just the bridge over Nitro Canyon and then the final straight to the finish line."

Suddenly... SCREEEEETCH!
Bolt, Roxy and Chunk slammed on their brakes. Yes, all three of them this time!

"No way! It's far too big and far too scary," shrieked Fizz. "Bolt should do it. The only reason he is lagging behind is because he kept helping everyone."

"OK Bolt," said Newton. "Based on the launch angle and the wind speed, you need to hit the ramp at 88 miles per hour."

Bolt was scared but he trusted Newton — he was the cleverest Monster in school. Bolt started racing towards the canyon...

ROARRRRR

"Yeeeeee - haaaaa!" screamed Bolt as he launched into the sky like a rocket.

"Come on Bolt!" the monsters cheered.

With wheels spinning, Bolt landed safely on the other side of the canyon and chased Masher towards the finish line.

On the final straight, it looked like Masher was going to win. **ROOOAAARR!** Bolt gave one more push and, to a huge cheer from the crowd, he overtook Masher and shot across the finish line in first place.

"Winning isn't everything," laughed Bolt. "But it does feel very nice. Especially with such great Monster Truck friends."

MONSTER TRUCKS

BOLT

SPEED - 100

BRAINS - 72

POWER - 65

SKILL - bravery

Bolt loves nothing more than racing and will do anything for his monster mates – except their homework!

MONSTER TRUCKS

FIZZ

SPEED - 99

BRAINS - 65

POWER - 30

SKILL - fast loop-the-loops

Step aside, here's Fizz! Small but speedy, Fizz is three-time winner of the Trucksville Drift & Style Cup.

MONSTER TRUCKS

NEWTON

SPEED - 95

BRAINS - 100

POWER - 42

SKILL - speaks 60 languages

Newton's brain is more powerful than a top-notch computer and he has a stylish crash helmet.

CHUNK

SPEED - 91	
BRAINS - 22	
POWER - 100	
SKILL - pie-eating champion	

Everyone loves Chunk! His brain is the size of a ping pong ball but he has a heart of pure gold.

ROXY

SPEED - 98	
BRAINS - 89	
POWER - 64	
SKILL - skatepark champion	

Streetwise Roxy is the queen of the skatepark and can successfully land a triple backflip.

MASHER

SPEED - 100	
BRAINS - 67	
POWER - 76	
SKILL - cheeky pranks	

Loud, fast and rather smelly, Masher is everyone's favourite bad boy. But not when he bends the rules…

The End